Busy Dog
Bonnie

Books About Bonnie:

BUSY DOG
Bonnie

BEL MOONEY

Illustrated by Sarah McMenemy

**WALKER
BOOKS**

First published 2009 by Walker Books Ltd
87 Vauxhall Walk, London SE11 5HJ

This edition published 2013

2 4 6 8 10 9 7 5 3 1

Text © 2009 Bel Mooney
Illustrations © 2009 Sarah McMenemy
Photo page 87 © Robin Allison-Smith

This book has been typeset in StempelSchneidler

Printed and bound in Great Britain by Clays Ltd, St Ives plc.

British Library Cataloguing in Publication Data:
a catalogue record for this book is available from the British Library

ISBN 978-1-4063-5119-4

www.walker.co.uk

For Luke Nicolic
B.M.

For my lovely son, Theo
S.M.

❖ Dolly Dog ❖

"It's funny," said Harry, "how you look forward to the school holidays and think you're going to be really busy all the time and then…"

"Yeah. It gets boring," sighed Zack.

The boys were sprawled on a pile of cushions in Zack's sitting room. They'd just switched the television off, because even watching TV gets tiring in the end. So does playing computer games. And raiding the biscuit tin again.

"We could put Bonnie in the garden and get her to chase the chickens," suggested Zack.

Harry shook his head. "No way – last time she got into trouble because they stopped laying."

Bonnie was curled up in a ball on one of the cushions, but she heard her name and raised her head.

"Come on, Bons," pleaded Harry. "Do something to make us laugh."

"I just have to *look* at your girly little dog to laugh," said Zack.

Harry wasn't sure he liked that. "What d'you mean?" he demanded.

Just then Zack's twin, Zena, came into the room. "Look at you two," she said, "lolling about doing nothing! I've tidied my room and found all sorts of bits and pieces I thought I'd lost, and I've made a pile of things I'm going to give Susie 'cos they don't fit me any more, and look – I've found all my old dolls' clothes." She held up an overflowing shoebox and smiled. "I thought Mum had given them to the charity shop. I'm going to sort them out now."

Zack made a face. "What a *busy* sister," he said in a not very nice voice.

But Harry secretly thought that Zena was having more fun than they were.

She sat down and tipped out the dolls' clothes. Right away Bonnie jumped up and ran over, seizing a tiny shoe in her mouth and shaking it – *"Grrrrrr"* – to and fro. The shiny black shoe shot out of her mouth, and when Bonnie went rushing after it, she tripped over the pile of dolls' clothes and ended up in a tangled heap.

"Bonnie wants to play dressing-up," laughed Zena.

"Now *that's* an idea!" shouted Zack.

"She's not going to like it," warned Harry.

"Course she will – she's a girl!" said Zack.

Bonnie was growling and twirling around
 and scattering the clothes and tossing little shoes in the air and nearly *killing* a doll's straw hat.

When Zena tried to stop her,
the fierce growls just got
louder.

"Grrrrr ... grrrrr ... grrrrr."

Zack rummaged in the
pile and picked out a skirt
with pink and white
polka dots.

"This is cool!"

he grinned.

Harry found a
tiny white bonnet.
"Check this out!"
"Oh, yes.
And what
about
keeping her
paws warm?" called
Zena, waving two blue
and white striped socks
in the air.

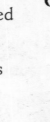

Now one of the best things about Maltese dogs is that they're very playful. Bonnie thought it a great game to be chased all around the room by three children waving dolly clothes, especially as she could run faster than they could. But in the end they cornered her among the cushions and – despite her wriggles – dressing-up time began.

Zena pulled a pink T-shirt over her head. Zack couldn't stop laughing as he added the pink and white skirt.

Harry tied the bonnet under her chin and murmured, through giggles, "Lucky you're so patient, Bons."

Then Zena put the blue and white striped socks on her front paws, but although they searched they couldn't find another pair. So they made do with one white sock and one red sock on Bonnie's hind legs – and she was finished.

The children fell about laughing, but Bonnie didn't mind. She raced around in circles, trying to shake the bonnet off. Then she tried to bite the socks, and the more the friends laughed, the more excited she got.

"I think you're the prettiest, girliest dog in England," spluttered Harry at last.

"No – the world," said Zena, scooping Bonnie up to cuddle her on her knee.

A few minutes later Zack looked at his watch and realized it was time for his favourite TV programme: a survival show. It took a while to find the remote under all the cushions, but soon they were watching it. Each week a former army sergeant showed how he could survive in the wild: building a shelter in a gale, lighting fires without matches, catching and cooking his own food.

"I wouldn't want to do that," said Harry. "I couldn't *kill* something."

"You would if you were hungry enough," argued Zack. "I mean, you'd eat your own dog if you had to."

"Never!"

On the screen the explorer was skinning an eel to cook over his campfire.

"Yuck," said Zena, covering her eyes.

Harry wanted to look away too, but he made himself watch so that Zack didn't accuse him of being *girly*.

The sitting room door opened and Zack and Zena's dad strode into the room, calling out, "Hello, gang!" Simon Wilson was tall and always cheerful, and worked in an office at home. Harry often felt a bit jealous that Zack and Zena had him around all the time, when his own dad lived far away in London with his girlfriend, Kim.

"Oh, I love this programme," Mr Wilson said, settling down to watch. "Look at him! That's the life, isn't it?"

"I'd rather eat cake than eel," said Zena. Her father hadn't even noticed the dressed-up dog on her lap.

"That's cos you're a *girl*," said her brother scornfully. "I'd eat *anything*. I'd be just as hard as him."

"Me too," said Harry.

"Yeah, right, Zack. Except you moan if Mum leaves your bedroom window open at night," Zena jeered.

"I do not! I wouldn't even mind if it snowed, because then I'd just dig myself into a hole to keep warm," Zack shouted.

"I remember going camping when I was a teenager," said Mr Wilson with a dreamy look in his eyes. "We had such a great time. Out there under canvas, with the night sky above you, the wind whistling in the trees. You really feel you're in touch with nature…"

By now the TV explorer was cleaning his hands in an icy cold stream and explaining how sometimes, in the army, they went for weeks without being able to wash.

"Sounds good to me," said Zack.

"My dad used to go camping too," Harry said quietly, almost to himself. "He told me he went all over France and Italy with a backpack and a tent."

"Cool!" said Zack. "Hey, maybe he'd take *us*!" He bounced around the room, full of the buzz of his big idea. "Yeah, Haz, ring your dad and see if he'll take you and me on a camping holiday."

"And me!" called Zena, but her brother ignored her.

"Go on, Haz – phone him!" insisted Zack.

Harry wished his friend would sit down again. "Look, he's going to catch that frog," he said, pointing at the TV. He wanted more than anything else to change the subject. He knew his dad would never have the time to take them on holiday. Or rather he wouldn't want to *make* the time. He had a new life now. "I wonder what frogs taste like?" he murmured.

Mr Wilson was watching him closely. "I know what," he said at last. "Why don't we find out? Why don't *I* take you camping?"

"Yay!" yelled Zack, and punched his fist in the air. "That's *sooooo* cool, Dad! We'll have a real adventure."

"We'll cook sausages and bacon over a fire…"

"…and wrap potatoes in foil to cook them as well!" added Zack.

"I've still got my old tent," said Mr Wilson, "and, if I remember rightly, it's huge. We'll have to buy a gas stove to cook on, but there's two sleeping bags in the attic."

"I've got my own," said Harry proudly. "My dad sent it last birthday."

"We'll need camp beds," said the twins' dad.

"What?" Zack folded his arms. "No way! On TV they just sleep on the ground. We've got to do it properly, Dad. We've got to be survivors!"

"Does that include eating eels?" Zena smiled. "I can't say I fancy that."

"Doesn't make any difference, 'cos *you're* not coming," said Zack spitefully.

There was a brief silence. Bonnie must have sensed trouble in the air, because she chose that moment to pop her head up from Zena's lap.

Mr Wilson spotted her and threw back his head to laugh. "What on earth's *that*? I thought you had one of your old dolls in your lap, love."

"Dad! You know I'm too old for dolls," Zena protested.

20

"Not too old to dress up a dog," said Zack.

"You dressed her up too!" she retorted.

Bonnie sat up and stretched. She looked so funny in the bonnet and clothes that Mr Wilson's laughter doubled. It was impossible for the children not to join in.

Phew! Harry thought. There goes the Bonnie effect again. She's stopped the quarrel.

But it wasn't going to be that easy.

"What's this about me not coming camping?" Zena demanded.

"Look, we're going to be out there in the dark, with the owls hooting and the wind howling – it'll be no place for a girl. You'd be terrified!" said Zack.

"No, I would not."

"Yes, you would."

"Hey, kids, wasn't this supposed to be a *fun* plan?" protested their father.

"What do you think, Haz?" asked Zack.

Harry cringed. Because he lived with
his mum, he liked the idea of going away
with Mr Wilson and Zack and it being a
boys' trip. But he didn't want to hurt Zena's
feelings by saying so.

The twins were both waiting. What could
he say?

"Er … what about Bonnie? Would she be
able to come?"

"You must be joking, Haz! No way!" said
Zack.

"Why not?" Zena asked.

They all stared at the tiny white dog
sitting innocently beside Zena. In the
bonnet, T-shirt, skirt and socks she looked
ridiculous.

"*That's* why," said Zack simply. "She's a
doll, not a dog."

Now Harry knew this really wasn't fair,
and he wanted to defend the small creature
who'd made such a difference to his life,

and to Mum's. But he also knew Zack hadn't really meant to insult her; he just wanted the camping trip to be for boys.

And Harry wanted that too.

"OK," he said at last. "I agree Bonnie shouldn't come. She doesn't like being outside all the time, and she might even get attacked by a fox. Tell you what, Zena, you could help Mum look after her that weekend. All you girls could hang out together?"

"Weekend?" said Zack. "I think we should go for a whole week!"

"Wow," said Zena. "Now I *know* I don't want to come. And nor does Bons."

Gently, head down, she started to take the dolls' clothes off Bonnie. Coal-black eyes looked up at her, knowing she was upset.

Bonnie knew what to do. She jumped up and licked Zena's face, so she shrieked "Yuck!" and fell backwards. Harry pulled her up, and together they chased Bonnie – still wearing all four socks – around the sitting room.

"Return of the racing rabbit!" shouted Zack. "Run your socks off, Bons!"

"Funniest dog in the world," chuckled Mr Wilson. "Now, boys, we've got to make plans. Lists. Camping keeps you really busy, you know."

Harry swept Bonnie up in his arms, and felt the excited beating of her heart matching his own.

"This is going to be the best holiday ever," he said.

BONNIE listened to Harry telling Mum the great plan and was glad she didn't fuss about it too much. They were all sitting at the kitchen table, Bonnie on Harry's knee. She could still taste the chicken and vegetable dog food she'd had for supper, and felt full and contented.

But for one thing.

Bonnie knew her job in life was to look after Harry and his mum — her very own pack. But Harry was talking about going into the wild countryside and sleeping in a field! Imagine what dangers he might meet!

Dress me up in dolly clothes, indeed! thought Bonnie. I'll show them what a girly dog is made of.

Yes, it was time she started making her *own* plans.

Stowaway Dog

It was the big day and Mr Wilson's car was filling up. The two mums brought out boxes of food and juice, while Mr Wilson packed his enormous old tent in the boot.

"I hope all the pieces are there," said Mrs Wilson. "It's a bit ancient."

"Just like you, Dad," grinned Zack.

The sun was shining, Bonnie was rushing around busily at their feet, and Harry felt happy. He brought out his rucksack and told his mother to stop worrying about the number of jumpers he was taking.

"This is summer, Mum!" he said. "It's warm!"

"Have you got torches?" asked Rosie Wilson. "And matches and firelighters?"

"And enough pans and a tin opener and a washing-up bowl and washing-up liquid?" added Harry's mum.

"And a sharp knife for skinning the eels and gutting the rabbits?" teased Zena.

"We've got everything but the kitchen sink!" said Mr Wilson cheerfully. It certainly looked like it.

There was hardly room in the car for the two boys.

Mr Wilson studied the map. "I reckon it'll take us about an hour and a half to get there," he said. "Then we'll have to find somewhere to camp and set up before dark."

"Won't you stay in a proper campsite?" asked Harry's mum in a worried voice.

"Oh no – it's out in the wilds for us guys!" said Mr Wilson.

"Yay!" shouted the boys.

Nobody was watching Bonnie. There was such a rush and a fuss and a bundling and a laughing and a shouting of goodbyes that Harry forgot all about his little dog. And his mum was so busy trying to hide the hint of a tear because her son was leaving

her for a *whole week* that she too failed to
notice where the little dog had gone. She
went back indoors, put the kettle on and
cut herself a slice of cake for comfort before
deciding the flat was too quiet without
the radio on – and only then did she look
around and call, "Bonnie?"

Mr Wilson and the boys were bowling
towards the motorway. Zack sat in the
front next to his dad; Harry was squashed
in the back, along with a pile of blankets,
cushions and sleeping bags. He gazed out of
the window, brimming with excitement that
they were finally on the way to their boys'
own adventure.

Minutes passed. Suddenly, without
warning, he felt strange.

He was being watched.

Slowly he turned his head – and saw two
small black beady eyes fixed on him.

"Oh, no! What on earth are *you* doing here?" he gasped.

Zack twisted round. "What? Who…?"

Bonnie poked her head out from the blankets and cushions. No one had seen her jump into the car and nestle down in the pile. Harry was sure her little mouth was smiling at him and asking, "So what are you going to do now?"

Which was exactly what Zack said. He didn't sound too pleased about their stowaway.

But Mr Wilson shrugged as he drove. "It doesn't matter. It's too late to take her back;

and anyway, it might be fun to have a dog along after all."

Harry phoned his mum to tell her what had happened. He promised everything would be fine. Bonnie crept along the seat and on to Harry's lap. He was glad to cuddle her soft fur, and he realized how much he'd have missed her.

"Well," he said, "she did survive being tied to a tree and abandoned, and she proved how brave she is in London, so she's not really a girly dog at all."

"Welcome on board, Wild Wabbit," said Zack.

It seemed for ever before Mr Wilson left the motorway, drove for a while longer, pulled into a lay-by to look at the map and told them, "Time we found ourselves a nice field."

It wasn't quite as easy as that. He'd decided they should be near a stream if possible, and there should be trees "for shelter from the sun", and of course they didn't want to be within sight of any houses. But at last they found the most beautiful spot.

"Look at that," said Mr Wilson, pointing to a field sprinkled with wild flowers. A stream tinkled over stones, and there was a clump of trees in one corner. "It's perfect!"

By the time they had carried all
the stuff from the car to the field it was
late afternoon. Bonnie went backwards and
forwards with Harry until her legs ached,
so as soon as they stopped she curled up on
the blankets and fell asleep. Harry wished he
could do the same.

"First – the tent!" called Mr Wilson.
"Come on, guys, help me unpack it."

Soon there was a vast amount of creased
canvas spread out in front of them, as well
as a jumble of poles and tent pegs.

"Um … I *think* I can remember how it
goes," murmured Zack's dad.

34

But putting up the old tent was like trying to solve the most complicated puzzle in the world.

"It's been a long time since I did this," puffed Mr Wilson as he struggled to work it out. "There used to be an instruction book…"

"Some families have a nice modern tent that just springs up by itself," complained Zack, trying to screw two halves of a pole together.

"You get inside, Harry, and find the place in the roof where the pole fits," ordered Mr Wilson.

Harry obeyed, and Bonnie went with him. He poked around with the pole, found the hole and shouted, "Hold it there!"

But Zack didn't hear and went on tugging at the canvas.

"Owwww!" yelled Harry as the pole fell over, burying him and Bonnie in a heap of musty old green tent.

"Yip yip yip yip!" barked Bonnie as Harry trod on her paw.

As Harry and Bonnie struggled to escape from the collapsed tent, Zack started to laugh. "It looks like there's a monster inside there!" he spluttered, holding his sides.

By the time they'd worked out how to put up the tent, they *all* looked like monsters.

Bits of grass were stuck to Mr Wilson's forehead, Zack had black smears on his face, and Harry was grubby and hot.

"Now fetch me the tent pegs," said Mr Wilson.

Soon he was on his knees, hammering away.

"There's one missing," said Zack. "Did you check it before we left, Dad?"

Mr Wilson tutted in irritation, but didn't say anything. But busy Bonnie trotted off to explore, and within minutes returned with a short stick in her mouth. It was slightly pointed at one end.

"Perfect!" said Mr Wilson. "I'll soon sharpen this with the knife and it'll work a treat."

"That's what he does in the survival programme!" cried Zack.

"Clever Bons!" whispered Harry proudly.

At last the tent was up, and they piled their sleeping bags, cushions and blankets inside. Then Mr Wilson brought a folding camp bed from the car. He looked rather sheepish.

"I know you said we should sleep on the ground, Zack, but I felt like a bit of comfort at my age," he explained. "And I brought you both rubber sleeping mats in case the ground's a bit hard."

"That's for wimps!" said Zack sternly.

Harry was less sure. "It, er, might be better for Bonnie, though..."

The next job was very unexpected. Mr Wilson pulled a spade from the boot of the car. "So who's going to start digging?"

"Start digging what?" asked Zack.

"A toilet, of course!"

"Oh," said Harry. "I thought we'd just, you know, go in the bushes."

"That's fine, apart from when you do something that needs burying," explained Mr Wilson.

"Oh," said Harry again. "I hadn't thought of that."

"Each day we'll dig a fresh hole, really deep, then fill it in at night so everything's buried. This is a real camp!"

Harry held out his hand for the spade and walked a short way off, behind a tangle of brambles. Bonnie trotted ahead, nose down, smelling all the magical scents of the countryside.

"You won't be so keen to go sniffing around here soon, Bons," he muttered.

But Bonnie was excited. She had so many things to discover, and soon her paws were scrabbling eagerly as she started to search for the creatures that lived under the grass. Harry felt inspired, and started to dig too. By the time he returned

to the others – hotter than ever – he felt
they really were surviving in the middle of
nowhere. It was fun.

Mr Wilson had set up the camping stove
and connected the gas canister. Zack carried
the cardboard box full of pans and plates
from the car and put it under the tent canopy.

"We've got enough food for about two
days," Mr Wilson said, "then we'll go on
a foraging expedition. Maybe we'll hunt a
rabbit, or a deer…"

Harry looked horrified but Zack rolled his
eyes. "Yeah, right, Dad!"

"OK – well, we'll find a village shop," smiled Mr Wilson.

"Maybe there's a burger place somewhere near?" said Harry hopefully.

"You can survive a week without burgers, my lad," said Mr Wilson, waving a finger.

It was then that Harry realized something: they had no food for poor Bonnie. After all, she wasn't supposed to be there. Harry knew Maltese dogs were very fussy eaters – not like Labradors or collies, which would wolf down anything. Bonnie only liked one flavour of her special food for toy dogs, and only one sort of biscuit. She had no bowl either – and she was looking very thirsty. What would he do?

"Improvise!" declared Mr Wilson.

He sent the boys off to search for firewood because he said they'd need a fire once the sun went down. Harry took Bonnie

to the stream and was
pleased to see she
could easily reach the
clear water – which
she lapped up eagerly.
But that didn't solve the
bowl problem.

When he got back to the camp with an
armful of wood he had a brain wave. His
mum had made him bring some plastic bags.
So he picked up Zack's baseball cap, lined
it with a plastic bag, and hey presto: a bowl
for Bonnie.

Mr Wilson clapped. "Brilliant! That's what
I call creativity!"

Zack looked down at his precious cap.
"That's what I call a liberty!" he retorted.

But nothing could spoil the buzz they all
felt as the sun went down, and Mr Wilson
made their fire and the four of them sat
around on blankets watching it crackle.

Bonnie cuddled
up next to Harry, gazing at the flames.
"This is the life, eh, lads?"

Harry wrapped small potatoes in foil and Mr Wilson showed him how to push them into the hot ashes. Then they started to cook the sausages and heat up beans. Bonnie sniffed the air. The sausages smelled good.

It didn't matter that the potatoes were just a bit hard, or that the sausages were burnt on one side. They all ate quickly, thinking that this was the best dinner they had eaten in ages, and Harry fed bits of sausage to Bonnie, who gobbled them up hungrily.

When the meal was over, and they'd stacked the plates and pans in the washing-up bowl to tackle in the morning, Mr Wilson fetched his battered old guitar from the car. "This is what we used to do when I was a student," he said, softly strumming the strings. "Now – what songs do we know?"

"'We Are the Champions'!" called Zack.

And as they all joined in, Bonnie jumped up on her hind legs, as if dancing for joy.

BONNIE snuggled against Harry and tried to get comfortable. This wasn't as good as his soft bed and she felt cold. How could Harry sleep? But he looked so tired after all the excitement that she guessed nothing could wake him. Not even that strange, unearthly shriek in the blackness outside.

Bonnie pricked up her ears. What *was* it? And then she heard:
"Twoo ... twoo ... twoo..."

Harry stirred and rolled over in his sleeping bag. Zack breathed heavily. Mr Wilson gave a little snore. But Bonnie was alert. She knew it was up to her to protect them from whatever was out there.

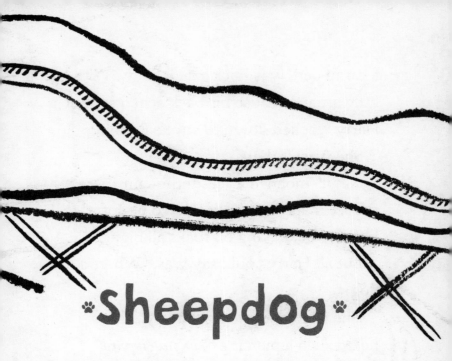

Sheepdog

In Harry's dream something big, mean and strong had been pummelling him until his whole body ached. And now the scary creature was still here, *breathing*. Just by his head. It gave a little cough – like no cough he had ever heard. What kind of monster could it be, to beat him up in the night?

He opened his eyes. Where was he?

Above him was green canvas; beside him was his best friend, Zack; and, raised up on a camp bed, was Zack's dad. Phew. With a little groan because his back ached so much, Harry reached down to stroke Bonnie.

She wasn't there.

"Ow!" moaned Zack. "I thought these rubber mats were supposed to be soft. I feel like I've been lying on rocks all night."

But all Harry could say was, "Where's my dog?"

The answer came right away. They heard such a piercing *"Yip yip yip yip!"* Harry thought he might die of shock. Something was out there and Bonnie was taking it on.

He was outside first, crouching under the awning, while Mr Wilson and Zack poked their heads through the opening behind him. In front of them was the most astonishing sight. During the night the field had completely filled up with sheep! They crowded around the tent like ghosts in the

pale light of morning, and every now and
then one coughed.

"Yip yip yip yip YIP!" yelped Bonnie. The
little dog stood in defensive mode: front legs
slightly bent, tail held high and hind legs
splayed out as she put all the energy of that
tiny body into her fiercest warning bark.

Standing in a wide circle, the sheep stared
in confusion, wondering what on earth this
thing was. After all, it was small, white
and fluffy like a lamb, but no lamb
had *ever* made a racket like that.

yip
yip
yip yip

They shuffled nervously. Right in the middle of the flock was an old ram, who decided that this noisy creature needed to be put in its place before it frightened all his girlfriends. He made a threatening run towards Bonnie, who stood her ground and gave a low growl.

"Grrrr-rrrrr … *grrrrr*!"

The ram replied with an equally warning "Meh-eh-*ehhhh*!"

Bonnie glared at the ram.
The ram glared back
at Bonnie.

Grrrrrr

"Good Lord,
it's fluffy creatures at dawn,"
laughed Mr Wilson. "This
stand-off could go on for hours."

As he moved out of the tent, the flock fled, including the ram. And it was then that they saw the mess the sheep had made. The washing-up bowl had been tipped upside down and one of their three plates was broken. A nosy ewe had nudged over their food box and the remains of the sliced bread lay scattered across the field. Their second packet of sausages had disappeared.

"I expect a fox or badger took them in the night," sighed Mr Wilson. "Thank goodness we brought lots of tins."

"Wow – a fox or badger!" said Zack.

"Wow-wow-ow-ow-ow!" said Bonnie.

"We're surrounded by *wild* things!" laughed Harry.

But just at that moment, the wildest thing of all came rushing across the field towards them, shouting, "Oi!"

"Uh-oh," whispered Mr Wilson, "I think this might be the farmer."

The man had
a red face that
looked as if it was
redder than usual
– with rage. He
waved a stick
and yelled, "You
there, stop that hound
from worrying my sheep!"

"What hound?" asked
Harry, clutching Bonnie,
who looked as if she couldn't
even worry a mouse.

"That there apology for a
dog of yours!"

"She was only barking to keep them away
from the tent," said Mr Wilson calmly.

"Aye! And that tent's got no business in
my field either! You're trespassing!"

It hadn't occurred to the boys that you
can't just camp wherever you like.

Zack looked up at his father, as if to say, "Come on, Dad, *you* got us into this!"

Very politely Mr Wilson explained that they hadn't known there would be sheep coming into the field; and they were really sorry, but they hadn't meant any harm. The farmer seemed to calm down a little. He muttered that when he'd let the sheep in at dawn he hadn't noticed the green tent under the trees.

"But I can't let you stay," he continued. "Don't you have a list of proper campsites?"

They shook their heads.

"You'll still have to go," he said firmly. "I'll give you a few hours to pack up, but I want you gone by this afternoon. Sorry now, but that's my last word. And mind you keep that mongrel under control."

And he stomped off across the field.

"Mongrel?" spluttered Harry indignantly. "Bonnie's a pedigree Maltese!"

He and Zack sat down dejectedly. Mr Wilson filled the kettle and put it on the gas stove to boil.

"All that setting up…" moaned Zack, looking around at their campsite.

The sky was grey and it wasn't as warm as yesterday. Harry ached all over from his night on the hard ground, and secretly he decided that camping was quite hard work.

"Cereal?" asked Mr Wilson in his most cheerful voice.

They started on breakfast and tried to work out what to do. Bonnie stared over at the sheep who were huddled in the furthest corner of the field.

"This is all Bonnie's fault," grumbled Zack. "He must have heard her barking. They probably heard her in America! I'm not being mean or anything, Haz, but she wasn't even supposed to be here."

"I know," Harry said miserably.

Bonnie snuggled in under his arm. She knew he was unhappy.

"Well, there's no rush," said Mr Wilson in the same jolly voice. "Look, we've still got eggs and bacon; I vote we cook breakfast and relax for a while."

"We've only got two plates now – and no bread," Zack grumbled.

"It doesn't matter; you can share mine," said Harry. He could see that Mr Wilson wore a disappointed face behind the cheery one.

But first they had to wash up, which meant boiling another kettle. It was tiring doing everything kneeling down, and the grass was damp. So were their sleeping bags, Harry discovered, when he went into the tent to tidy up. By the time Mr Wilson had finished cooking the eggs the bacon was cold, and they realized they'd forgotten the ketchup. Harry wished he could put it all in a sandwich so Zack could have the plate.

"This is the life, eh?" said Zack's dad, wrapping his hands around his mug of tea in an attempt to warm them up.

Harry gave Bonnie a small piece of bacon but she spat it out.

The boys didn't think much of Mr Wilson's suggestion that they all wash their faces and clean their teeth in the stream.

"It's freezing!" Zack protested, but his father insisted.

For a few minutes, as he splashed his face with the icy grey water, Harry thought longingly of the nice cosy bathroom at home, with Mum's pots of cream on the shelf – but he pushed the image away. This was their boys' adventure and they would just have to get used to it.

After they'd finished getting ready, and waited for another kettle to boil so they could wash up breakfast this time, it was nearly eleven; but there was still no sign of the sun which had made yesterday so perfect. Harry rummaged in his rucksack for his extra jumper.

Rooks cawed in the trees. It was a wild, harsh sound, Harry thought with a shiver – not like the "meeehs" and "baas" from the sheep, which were oddly peaceful. He gazed across the field, trying not to hear Mr Wilson get cross with Zack because he was making a fuss about having to pack up and move on to find a proper campsite.

Once again he forgot to check where Bonnie was. That was the trouble with camping: it took a lot of time, attention and effort. There were no spare moments to play with a dog. But Bonnie liked to be busy, and this whole outdoor business was starting to bore her. The most exciting thing that had happened so far was meeting those sheep – so off she went to have another look. Maybe she'd bark at that old ram again.

She skirted the flock before they spotted her coming. This brought her to the very edge of the field, near the gate. But right away the little dog saw that something was wrong. The gate wasn't closed properly. For a second, she wanted to follow her instinct, to escape from that field and run all the way home to Mum. But Harry was here, so she had to stay put.

At that moment, the first sheep nudged against the gate and it opened a little wider. Sheep always follow each other, so in seconds the flock were crowding around the gateway to freedom. But Bonnie wasn't having that! If she couldn't escape from the field, then neither could these woolly things with silly faces. Quickly she ran through ahead of them, dodging their hooves, then turned to face the leader.

"*Yip yip yip yip YIP!*" she barked.

The old ram moved forward to stand next to the first ewe, and the pair of them took a couple of menacing steps towards Bonnie.

"YIP YIP YIP YIP *YIP!*"

The small dog stood at the edge of the lane, daring the flock to take one more step. On the other side of the field Harry looked up and started to run.

But just then an old car pulled up and a woman jumped out. She was wearing wellingtons and a green jacket, and carrying a stick.

"Hey!" she yelled, taking one look at Bonnie, and another at the sheep, before striding forward and shouting "Garn!" at the sulky-looking ram.

Bonnie stood her ground, barking her tiny head off, while the woman drove the flock back, then securely latched the gate. By this time Harry had arrived, with Zack and Mr Wilson close on his heels.

"I'm … I'm … really … s-sorry," he panted.

The farmer's wife (for that was who she was) smiled. "If this is your little dog, there's nothing to be sorry about," she said warmly. "That daft lot would've been halfway to the village, and no doubt munching people's gardens, if he hadn't kept them in."

"He's a she," Harry said.

"She's a sheepdog!" called Zack.

"Well, we could give her a job!" laughed the lady.

When she and Mr Wilson started to chat they concluded that her husband must have been so cross that morning, he'd failed to shut the gate properly.

"Typical!" she said. "Don't you worry now. I'll tell him how your little dog saved his precious sheep. You're welcome to camp in our field, and you can stay as long as you like!"

"Brilliant!" said Mr Wilson, rubbing his hands together. "So, boys, it's a long country walk today and then tinned mince and peas tonight!"

"Er … great," said Harry.

BONNIE fluffed up her fur in an attempt to keep warm. It was the middle of the night. Inside the tent it was freezing, and outside it was freezing *and* raining. *Pitter-patter, pitter-patter* went the drops on the canvas. There was a rumble of thunder, and not long afterwards the tent was lit up by a flash of light.

Bonnie could sense that Harry was awake. Even through the sleeping bag she could feel him shivering, and soon there was the sound of his teeth chattering.

She knew what she had to do. Centuries ago her ancestors had lived in castles that were bitterly cold. The little dogs had been kept for warmth and comfort as well as love. So Bonnie crept up to Harry's head and wormed her way down into his sleeping bag. Her furry body was much warmer than Harry's and he murmured, "Thank you, Little Bear".

Bonnie sighed happily as they settled down to sleep. Being a cosy hot-water bottle was just another part of looking after her little pack.

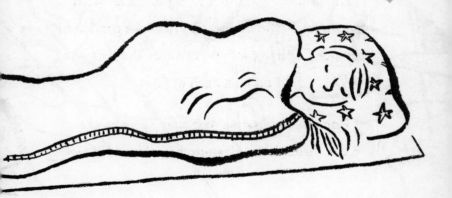

✸ RESCUE DOG ✸

"Well, team, the thing about a British summer is, it sorts out the men from the boys!" said Mr Wilson in the loudest, jolliest voice he had used so far (which was saying something). "This is our biggest test yet, but we'll survive!"

The three of them peered out of the tent at a world streaming with water. The field full of flowers had been transformed into a sea of mud. The sheep huddled miserably under the trees near by, and the air was heavy with their rich, damp, oily smell. The wind had blown rain in through the tent flap to form a puddle at the entrance. In it sat the toilet roll they'd left there so it could be easily reached when needed.

"That's … er … unfortunate," said Mr Wilson. "But never mind. I've got an old newspaper in the car."

Rivulets of rainwater had run in along the groundsheet and started to soak into Zack's sleeping bag. Worse, they had all left their boots outside the tent under the canopy, but it had blown to one side and they were also soaking wet.

"Lucky we brought our trainers too," said Mr Wilson brightly.

"Yeah, very lucky," said Zack in a flat voice.

"The cereal and milk are in here, so at least we can have breakfast," said Harry, trying to help Mr Wilson by sounding enthusiastic. But the cornflakes had given

up on crunchiness during the night. Harry
offered Bonnie one soaked in milk but the
little dog turned her head away.

"Tell you what we'll do today," said Zack's
dad. "We'll drive to the village and have a
slap-up pub lunch. How about that?"

"Cool!" said Harry.

"How long till lunchtime?" asked Zack,
jumping into Harry's empty sleeping bag
and snuggling down.

"We'll buy fresh supplies – and we can
get Bonnie some dog food too. Now she's
rescued our holiday by guarding the sheep,

we need to spoil her, don't we?" Mr Wilson reached out to pat Bonnie's head, but she ducked away.

"You're such a brave girl, aren't you?" Harry whispered. But Bonnie wouldn't look at him. He didn't understand it.

"So are we all OK with the plan?" Mr Wilson asked. "We've got to regroup, reorganize, rearm – just like soldiers! All onside, team?"

After a long pause the boys nodded wearily.

"Hmm, something tells me… But no, you wouldn't want to give up and go home, would you, boys?"

Zack thought of his sister and how she would tease them. Harry thought of his mum and how she would say she was right. Each knew he couldn't look at the other in case the secret was given away.

So they both chorused, "Of *course* not!"

Then everybody fell silent for a while, listening to the soft drift of rain on canvas and the bleating of the sheep. The tent seemed to get colder and colder, and Harry remembered his mum telling him to pack more jumpers.

Oh dear. That's the trouble with mums: they *are* always right.

"What d'you think the farmer's wife said to that poor old farmer last night?" asked Mr Wilson at last with a wink. "I bet she gave him a hard time!"

"Anybody who lives out *here* already has a hard time," said sulky Zack.

Harry was shocked. He'd never seen his friend like this and couldn't bear him to spoil things – not when Mr Wilson had been such a great dad to bring them camping. He thought back to the moment when Zack had suggested his own dad take them on holiday, and Harry had felt sad because he knew that would never happen. Mr Wilson had stepped in, been enthusiastic, dragged his old tent from the attic, loaded the car, driven them all the way out here…

Mr Wilson was a really special dad. Even if he wasn't the most experienced camper.

"I reckon she told the farmer to take Bons on as a sheepdog," Harry said brightly. "She's proved she isn't a girly dog at all."

"Well, she looks as if she could do with a few layers of dolls' clothes now," said Zack.

Harry followed his pointing finger and glanced down. Bonnie was shivering so much, it was as if last night's wind were still shaking the tent and everything in it. Her tail dragged on the ground and her ears drooped. When Harry reached to scoop her up she was as floppy as a soft toy.

"Hey, what's the matter, Mouse-Face?" he whispered.

Now, what most people don't realize about dogs is that while their job in life is to be devoted to us, they also need some very important things in return. If any dog could sit down and make a list, it would look something like this:

- Food.
- Companionship.
- Warmth and comfort.
- Security.
- Fun, games and attention.

The point was, Bonnie wasn't getting *any* of those things in that tent. Usually she could tell what Harry was feeling even before he could, but today he was trying to hide his real mood from everyone – including her. And it was keeping him so busy that he wasn't paying her proper attention. She knew Harry was telling fibs with every smile and every brave response, and that annoyed her because it shut her out. It was no fun. But then, how could you have fun and games in a wet tent?

But that wasn't the worst thing. She could do without the warmth, comfort, security, food and fun if only she had his companionship.

"Poor little dog," said Mr Wilson.

Hearing the concern in his voice, Bonnie made a point of shivering even more.

"I've never seen her like this," said Harry anxiously.

Now Bonnie bowed her head, like a dying flower.

"Do you think she's caught a chill?" asked Zack.

Bonnie let out a little mewing sound.

"Put her down and let's see how she looks," said Mr Wilson.

Harry set her down gently on the floor of the tent. Oh, you have never seen such a bedraggled sight! Bonnie's tail drooped, her tummy scraped the ground, her head was low, and when Harry whistled softly to get her to move she dragged her paws like a very old dog. And all the time she was quaking like a leaf in the wind.

"She really doesn't look well, does she?" said Mr Wilson.

"These little dogs can get ill very quickly," said Harry in a voice as small and drooping as his dog.

"Maybe we haven't been taking care of her very well," said Zack.

The three of them stared at Bonnie and, feeling their gaze, she responded by shivering even more. Then suddenly she flopped down on her side, paws outstretched.

"Argh! She's collapsed," Harry cried. "What are we going to do?"

"I know," said Zack. "We'll have to take her home!"

"It's not fair on the animal to keep her here," Mr Wilson agreed, "even though we *are* having such a great time ourselves."

"She probably needs the vet," whispered Harry, gently stroking her head, "but I'm sorry she's made us end our holiday early."

"That's *fine!*" Zack said cheerfully.

"Can't expect a toy dog to survive in the wild," said Mr Wilson, starting to roll up sleeping bags with enthusiasm.

"Got to put animals first," said Zack, stuffing clothes into his rucksack with a big grin. "They're not as strong as us."

"You'd better cuddle your pet and let me and Zack pack up," Mr Wilson told Harry.

Naturally, Harry had no choice but to agree.

Luckily the rain had stopped. It took no time at all to pack up, because nobody cared about doing things neatly. The tent was soaked and heavy, but Mr Wilson managed to fold it up and haul it to the car without putting it in its bag. Zack bundled together the poles and tent pegs any old how. Father and son became filthier and filthier – and more and more cheerful – as the site cleared and the car filled.

Meanwhile Harry wrapped Bonnie in a T-shirt and held her tight. Her eyes were closed. When he put his face down to hers she didn't even stick her tongue out to give him a lick.

The sheep watched curiously and the ram stamped his hooves every now and then, but it was as if the flock knew the annoying strangers and their yappy pretend lamb would soon be out of their field.

At last they were done.

"Just as well you've got us, Haz," said Zack importantly. "And make sure you tell my sis how we put your poor dog first."

Harry nodded. "Definitely."

"She couldn't have lasted another night – that's what I reckon."

"I'm sure you're right," said Harry, and wished they had a helicopter to whisk Bonnie home as quickly as possible.

Mr Wilson put the heater on in the car, and a good CD, and found some sweets, and the journey home seemed much faster than the journey out. But the strangest thing was this: as soon as they were on the way, Bonnie stopped shivering. She perked up so quickly, you'd have thought a miracle had happened.

Her tail went up.

She pricked up her ears.

Her eyes were bright.

She jumped up to give Harry a lick, and started a play fight with the corner of a blanket.

"I think she's feeling a bit better," said Harry at last.

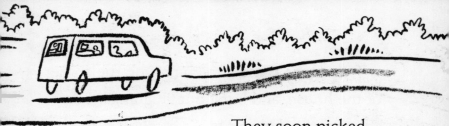

They soon picked
up a mobile phone signal,
and Zack rang his mum to tell her they
were coming home. Harry spoke to his mum
and begged her not to fuss over Bonnie.

But when they arrived in their street, and
the two mums ran out to greet them, nobody
would ever have thought the little dog had
been ill. She bounded around, greeting
Harry's mum as if she hadn't seen her for two
hundred years, instead of two nights.

"I think the damp got to her," Mr Wilson
told them.

"And of course, she was missing her
proper food and comfy bed," added Zack.

"I'm sorry we had to finish our adventure
early," said Harry.

"That's OK," chorused the Wilsons, father
and son.

Then Zena came strolling round the corner
of the house, and burst out laughing when
she saw her dad and brother caked in mud
from head to foot.

"Wow, you look like real soldiers!"
she said. "Was it tough
out there?"

Zack nodded. "It was *terrible*, very bad conditions."

"A real storm," added his dad.

"Bonnie was terrified," said Harry.

"We had to save her from a dangerous ram."

"We were running out of food."

The others listened in admiration. Then Mrs Wilson said she had shepherd's pie and peas ready, and Harry's mum went to fetch the chicken breast she had already cooked and cut up for Bonnie, and they all piled into the Wilsons' house.

Much later, when Harry and his mum were home and cuddled up on the sofa with Bonnie, Mrs Smith looked closely at the little dog and asked, "Was she really ill, Harry? She seems fine now."

"I know," he said, puzzled, "but honestly, Mum, she was shivering *so* badly. It was terrible!"

"Almost as terrible as the camping, eh, love?" she asked.

"How did you know?"

"I can read your mind, and I reckon Bonnie can too!"

"Don't tell anybody else, Mum – but yes," whispered Harry, relieved he could be truthful at last.

"Just as well we've got our very own rescue dog, Harry!'" laughed Mum.

BONNIE sighed happily. Oh, it was so good to be home. She felt full of chicken, and this was what she loved best of all: the three of them on the sofa — her pack cosy together.

Outside, it had started to rain again, but it didn't matter. Harry had played with her ever since they'd arrived. That was fun. And Mum had made such a fuss of her. That was proper attention. Just what she knew she deserved.

Tomorrow they'd go for a walk in the park, and there would be smells to sniff, other dogs to bark at, a ball to chase. And back at home there would be post to ambush when it came through the letter box, the doorbell to yelp at ... oh, so much to do!

Life was good when you were a busy dog, safe in your own home.

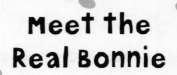

Meet the
Real Bonnie

Born: December 2001 or January 2002
(see Bonnie's Life Story on page 86).

Likes: Bel (best of all) – and the rest
of the family.

Dislikes: The postman – and anyone who
comes to the front door.

Hates: Being brushed and bathed.

Hobbies: Being cuddled, sleeping and going
for (short) walks.

Favourite job: Being Bel's bridesmaid.

Favourite food: Chicken and ham.

Favourite place: Sleeping on a red cushion with
"Love" written on it.

Favourite collar: The black one with diamonds
all round it.

Least favourite collar: The pale blue one
because it's too chunky.

Is mostly fed by: Bel's husband, Robin.

Is least spoilt by: Bel.

Is most spoilt by: Bel's parents (Bonnie thinks of them as grandparents).

Q: Can you write a fact-file for your special pet?

....

....

....

....

....

....

Bonnie's Life Story

Bel says:

I don't know when Bonnie was born because I didn't meet her until she was about six months old. She had been left tied to a tree in a park in the centre of Bath, where we live. How could anybody do that to a tiny dog? I don't know who found her. All I know is that she was

taken by the dog warden to the RSPCA Cats' and Dogs' Home – and then she came to live with me. The vet looked at her carefully and said she was very healthy and roughly six months old. Bonnie and I loved each other right from the beginning and lived happily ever after – just like Harry, his mum and the Bonnie in my stories.

Q: Who was the luckiest – Bonnie or Bel?

Q: Do you know anyone who has a pet from a rescue home? Do you know anything about its life story?

Bonnie's Star Sign

Astrology is the study of the stars and how the star sign you are born under can affect who you are and what happens to you. So is there such a thing as "Dogstrology"? Some people think so, because I've got a book on it! But I realized that because I don't know exactly when Bonnie was born, she could be one of two star signs.

Sagittarius (22 November – 21 December)
Adventurous • Optimistic • Jolly
Enthusiastic • Happy-go-lucky

Capricorn (22 December –19 January)
Steady • Patient • Determined
Trustworthy • Hard-working

Q: Which do you think sounds most like Bonnie? Can you work out your pet's star sign?

Aquarius (January 20 – February 18)

Pisces (February 19 – March 20)

Aries (March 21 – April 19)

Taurus (April 20 – May 20)

Gemini (May 21 – June 20)

Cancer (June 21 – July 22)

Leo (July 23 – August 22)

Virgo (August 23 – September 22)

Libra (September 23 – October 22)

Scorpio (October 23 – November 21)

Bonnie's Pet Names

Bons

Mouse

Rabbit

Little Bear

Squiggy

Fox-Face

Puppy

Pupple

Pets

Baby Girlfriend

Q: Which do you think sounds most like Bonnie?

Q: What funny names do you call your pet?

Q: What funny names do you call your best friends?

Q: What funny names do people call you?

Bonnie Dresses Up!

**Can you draw some funny outfits
for Bonnie?
Q: Which look would Bonnie like best?**

Love Bonnie? Then why not read all six of her tail-wagging adventures!

To find out more about the books and the real-life Bonnie who inspired them, visit belmooney.co.uk

Bel Mooney is a well-known journalist and author of many books for adults and children, including the hugely popular Kitty series. She lives in Bath with her husband and real-life Maltese dog, Bonnie, who is the inspiration for this series. Bel says of the real Bonnie: "She makes me laugh and transforms my life with her intelligence, courage and affection. And I just know she's going to pick out a really good card for my birthday."

Find out more about Bel at belmooney.co.uk

Sarah McMenemy is a highly respected artist who illustrates for magazines and newspapers and has worked on diverse commissions all over the world, including art for the London Underground, CD covers and stationery. She illustrated the bestselling City Skylines series and is the creator of the picture books *Waggle* and *Jack's New Boat*. She lives in London.

Find out more about Sarah at
sarahmcmenemy.com